NEVER ENOUGH

A Sussex Crime novella

ISABELLA MUIR

OUTSET PUBLISHING LTD

Published in Great Britain

By Outset Publishing Ltd

First edition published June 2022

ISBN: 978-1-872889-46-7

www.isabellamuir.com

Cover photo: Zoltan Tasi on Unsplash

CONTENTS

PRAISE FOR THE SUSSEX CRIME NOVELLAS

'A surprising Christmas-themed novella set in a period of great uncertainty.'

'This was a fabulous short story, capturing exactly the excitement of Christmas, and how it must have been at the start of the Second World War. Family is at the heart of the story, with two families whose children are friends.'

'Set during the Second World War this intriguing cozy crime mystery is perfect for dark winter evenings, delivering a satisfying conclusion to a well-written story.'

'...you are taken into the lives of the people who live in this small town near the sea in England during WWII.'

You can discover more about my books and characters on my website. www.isabellamuir.com

or follow me on Twitter: @SussexMysteries

ONE

THE CONFLICT IS INEVITABLE now. For months I've known there will be no way to stop it worming its way into my home, my family.

We have tried to shelter the children, but the evidence is all around. I guess they are old enough to hear the latest news when it comes. Philip, at least. I'd like Jessica to enjoy what's left of her normal childhood for just a little while longer. Soon nothing will be normal for any of us.

Family time, quiet pleasures will be a thing of the past, as the creeping fog of what is to come threatens to overshadow the sun. For me, at least. During this summer Helen and I spent many weekends on the beach, watching the children splashing in the waves. Grabbing at moments that will become memories to hold on to when the darkness descends. Conversations were light, unimportant, while unspoken words sat at the back of my throat like a sour tasting berry I was loath to bite into. I fixed my eyes on the pleasure our children found in the simplest of pastimes. Jessica, still young enough to want to build a sandcastle, Philip at that bullish age when he delights in knocking it flat.

Before we set off Helen filled a bag with sandwiches, fruit, and a flask of tea and we'd spread a blanket out on the shingle. Some days we needed to wrap the blanket around the children by the end of the afternoon when the wind whipped up and they shivered, partly from the cold and partly from exhaustion. All played out.

These were short, grabbed moments. The rest of it has been a summer of closing down and closing in. Both the play parks near to us in Tamarisk Bay now remind me more of the trenches of my nightmares than a place for my children to enjoy. Soil has been dug, shelters created, surrounded by sandbags, just waiting for terrified families to hide there when the air-raid sirens sound for real. The gas masks sit on our kitchen counter like some kind of strange animal invasion. I wish for nothing more than to put them into the dustbin, along with all the other unwelcome additions to our home. Taped windows and blackout curtains, the flask of water, tinned food and blankets kept in the understairs cupboard; our own attempt at a safe haven should the worst happen. All I can do is pack away memories of those carefree weekend afternoons and store them like tinned food, keeping them fresh until we can enjoy them again.

Helen comes through from the kitchen, two mugs of cocoa on a tray, accompanied by a plate of digestives. We exchange a look, but no words pass between us. It's coming up to nine. She sits and watches as I turn the wireless on, ready to hear the news broadcast. I turn the volume low. Helen and I sit either side of the dresser, both facing the brown wooden box from which emerges words to confirm the change we have been preparing for.

We've known about the evacuation plan for a while now. Operation Pied Piper. Children, as well as women who are in the family way, are to leave the cities to get them out of harm's way. Thousands of them will head for the coast or the countryside. Sussex is a designated reception area, with every family expected to take at least one child.

We sip our cocoa and listen to the detailed information. Trains and buses are being requisitioned, calls made to thousands of volunteers to help with the organisation. Some children will leave London on boats, travelling down the River Thames; a bizarre adventure but one that will take them to the unknown, a life with strangers.

The broadcast finishes and Helen sets her mug down on the footstool. 'It's time we told Philip and Jessica.'

I know she's right, but I know too that explaining the reasons behind this change to our family life will remove any possibility of normality for all of us. Children and young women are leaving cities because their homes will be bombed. There, it's said. There was a chance not so long ago when we all hoped politicians had succeeded in staving off the madness of another war. I remember the last one all too well and, despite being a non-believer, I have prayed every day that my children would never see such a conflict. Chamberlain returned from Munich with his promise of 'peace in our time', but Herr Hitler is determined. And so, in turn, we also need to be determined. The alternative is unthinkable.

Helen is speaking, her lips moving, but the thoughts in my head block out her words.

'Sorry, darling. Say that again, would you? I was miles away.'

She smiles and takes my hand in hers. 'There's space in Philip's room if we take in a boy, but what if it's a girl? We can hardly have her sleeping in with us. It's fine for Jess, but not for a stranger. I'm not sure how it's all going to work. What do you think? There's the box room, but I can't see how we'll fit a bed in there and with no window to look out of, the poor child will feel as though they're in a prison cell.'

I nod. There is an image in my mind, as though I am watching a film on the big screen. Soon I will rejoin my regiment. They have only called the young men so far, but I can't sit back and let others face the danger, even though the memories of my time in the trenches still haunt my nights. Soon they will haunt my days too.

'It's just families, isn't it?' Helen interrupts my thoughts again. I wait for her to explain. Her face is tight with concern, or maybe apprehension.

'They won't ask Bill Marchant, will they?'

'I doubt it. He can barely care for himself since Martha died.'

Bill Marchant lives on the west side of Tamarisk Bay, in a cottage he's lived for his whole life, by all accounts. Rumours spread through the town that his wife, Martha, had died seven days before they found her. The story was that he'd sat by her bedside day and night, hoping she'd wake up. It was only when Bill didn't visit to collect her pills that Dr Langley thought it best to investigate.

'You don't believe the rumours though, do you?' Helen asks.

'What, that he had a hand in her death?'

Helen nods, a frown tightening across her forehead.

'No charges were brought. The poor woman had been ill for years. And we've always said we won't listen to rumours. Or at the very least, if we listen we shouldn't heed them.' I say, standing and holding my hand out to Helen. 'Bed?'

Helen takes both mugs through to the kitchen. I turn off the lights and follow her upstairs. It's a nightly routine that we have followed since Philip was born. I wait while she opens his bedroom door a crack, closes it again, then moves down the landing to our room. A curtain hangs across the middle of the room, beyond which our daughter is sleeping soundly.

'Please God we'll all have a chance to sleep soundly for a good while yet,' I say, knowing my mention of the Almighty will come as a surprise to my wife. She has always been a believer and now I almost envy her that.

Once in bed, I pick up the book I have been attempting to read for weeks, never getting past the first dozen pages. I know as I move through the story that Brighton Rock will speak of violence and anger. I should take it back to the library and choose another tale, one that doesn't resemble a world we are about to fall into, and yet somehow I hold on to a hope that when I reach the end – if I ever reach the end – goodness will triumph. Not just on the pages of a work of fiction, but in real life, in the world around me.

'What do you think about the rooms?' Helen holds her book in front of her, but it remains closed.

'Whatever you think is best,' I say.

'What's best is that these poor children can stay with their families, but that's not going to happen, is it?'

There is an edge to her voice.

'You never hear of a woman starting a war, do you?' She looks straight ahead as if addressing some unknown aggressor.

'I hate it as much as you.'

'But you'll go and fight, won't you? If everyone just said, no. No to war. Maybe we could live our lives in peace.'

'You're being naïve. The world doesn't work like that.'

She's not angry with me, not really. And yet when she puts her unopened book back on the bedside table and turns off her reading light, there's a heavy weight in the pit of my stomach. The heaviness increases when she turns her back to me, tugging the bedspread up around her shoulders; a physical barrier.

'I didn't make the world the way it is,' I say, hearing a childishness in my voice that reminds me of my son when I've accused him of some misdemeanour that he promises he has never committed.

Helen chooses not to reply. I want to talk it through, to explain my side of the argument, if it is an argument. But I know my wife. Her response to any disagreement between us is silence, the hardest thing of all to rail against.

'It's my duty to protect you and the children and if that means I wage war on our enemy, that's what I'll do.' I know she's listening and so I continue. 'What kind of man would I be if I stayed at home while thousands who are no more than boys are prepared to sacrifice their lives? What kind of husband and father would that make me?'

'You'd be alive.' She whispers the words into the bedcover.

I understand her anger stems from fear. Fear that when I rejoin my army regiment she won't see me again. Or that if I come home I'll be missing a limb, or disfigured beyond recognition. Fear too that while I am gone she will be both mother and father to our children, that it will be her alone who must keep them safe. And now an extra responsibility. Another child loaned to us for safekeeping.

I tug at her shoulder, encouraging her to turn towards me, which she does, nestling her head on my chest.

'You'll be just fine,' I say, brushing my lips against her hair that smells of lavender water. 'We'll decide on the sleeping arrangements together. Tomorrow. After we tell the children.'

'You're never going to read that book, are you?' She takes it from me and leans across me to put it on my side table.

'I need it to have a good ending, but I'm doubtful it will work out that way.'

'The book, or our lives?' She looks up at me, the shadow from my reading light catching the tightening lines around her eyes.

'I love you,' I say, turning out the light and holding her close, willing sleep to come soon, although I fear it will elude me for some time yet.

HELEN

I'm relieved when daylight starts to seep through the slight gap at the edge of the blackout curtains. It's a little after five o'clock, but I've been awake for an hour or more, lying still so as not to disturb George. He will wake soon enough, but before that I like the children to be up and breakfasted. It means that at weekends at least he can have his breakfast in peace. He's never been good with noise early in the day.

Down in the kitchen, I fill the kettle and set it on the hob. Running cold water into the kitchen sink I wash my face, then take a flannel for a quick freshen up. I don't mind the cold in the morning. It helps wake me up and means I can save the hot water for George's shave and a pot of tea for us all.

Philip is first down, the sleep in his eyes making him seem younger than his fourteen years. He takes after his father, choosing to be quiet first thing, saying little. He has yet to work a Saturday shift at the sorting office, leaving him free to help with chores, which he does without my asking.

'I'll get more coal in, shall I?' His fringe falls down across his face as he takes a bite of the buttered bread.

'I need to cut that fringe.' As I run my fingers through his hair, he pulls away a little. I remember my surprise when they handed my firstborn to me. A shock of dark hair that turned to thick curls by the time he was toddling. Something his sister is certain to envy when she spends so much time with her friend Lucy, plaiting each other's hair, trying desperately to alter their straight locks.

'What else needs doing, Mum? Ronnie finishes work at midday, so I promised him we'd meet up for a bike ride later.' With his breakfast finished in no more than half a dozen bites, he puts the crockery into the sink and heads for the back door.

'Wait until Jessica is down, and your father. We need to talk to you about something.'

'Is it about the evacuees?' He tosses out the word as if it has always fitted into everyday conversation, and yet for me it is a word that signals a change to our lives that fills me with apprehension. Adding another child to our family isn't the problem, it's all that goes along with it.

'What do you know about it?'

'Everyone's talking about it. They're being sent out of London, aren't they? Otherwise they'll all be bombed. But what about the people left behind? What about the old people? Don't they matter?'

Youthful indignation is writ large across his face and it makes me sad. I can't save him from the realisation that the world is not a fair place.

'Don't make too much of it when we tell Jessica. I don't want her scared.'

'Jess will only be worried about someone touching her things. She won't give a thought to how hard it will be for someone coming to live with strangers. Mum, it could be us having to go away. Imagine that.'

He's wise beyond his years.

'You're a good boy, Philip. Now help me get your father's breakfast ready and then, yes, if you can fill the coal scuttle, it'll be ready for later. Although we shouldn't need a fire this evening, if it chills down we can always put on another jumper.'

I turn to run some water into a bowl, ready to wash the breakfast things, when I hear my daughter's footsteps on the stairs.

'Dad's snoring,' she says as she enters the kitchen. 'And he was snoring most of the night. Mum, when are we going to empty the box room so I get to have my own bedroom? I'm too old to be sleeping in with you two. I am nine, you know.'

Jessica swings between irritation that life isn't treating her the way she expects and a dream state where she floats around in a world fired by her imagination. I can't guess how she will take the news that the four of us are soon to be joined by another child who will inevitably compete for my time and attention.

'We need to talk about sleeping arrangements. But for now have your breakfast quickly before Dad comes down so he can have his breakfast in peace.'

An hour later George is up, shaved and fed and the kitchen has been returned to order. The children have wandered into different parts of the house, Philip back up into his bedroom and Jessica into the garden, after announcing that she wants to 'look for bees'.

'Do you want to tell them, or would you rather I do it?' I ask my husband, as he turns the pages of the newspaper in such a way that I doubt he is reading a word.

'Don't make a big fuss. Say it's something that is going to happen and not just to us, to all families. You pander too much to them, Helen. How they feel about it is neither here nor there.'

'You won't admit that you worry about them as much as I do.'

'This is no time for an argument. You'll need to be down at the station by midday.'

'I'll need to be at the station? You're not coming with me?'

'Children like to see women's faces, someone to remind them of their mothers. I'll be here when you come back.'

Just before noon, the three of us walk to the railway station. Philip ahead of me, Jessica dawdling behind. I revisit our conversation of earlier, my failed attempts at reassuring my young daughter that all would be well.

'But why do they have to live with us? We don't even have enough space for me to have a proper bedroom,' she said.

Philip tried to assuage her. 'Jess, just think about what it's going to be like for them. They're leaving their family. They don't even know when they'll see them again.'

'And what if they've got nits? I'm not sharing a room with anyone who has nits and that's it. I'll run away if you make me.' By now she is so fired up that I can see our discussion ending in tears.

'Jessica, not every child who lives in London has nits,' I tell her.

'But there are slums in cities, everyone knows that. And slums are dirty and that's why there are nits.' She stated it as unquestionable fact.

'What about last winter? Someone in your class had nits. Didn't they just live down the road, not in a slum, not in a city?' I felt as though I was gravitating to ridiculous arguments, when there was no need for any argument at all.

'That was Sarah Spencer. She smells, everyone knows that.'

'Now you're being unkind. If Sarah smells and I'm sure she doesn't, but if she does it might be because her family has even less space in their house than we do, it's doubtful her poor mother can manage a weekly bath for all of them. Hasn't Sarah got five brothers?'

Jessica stormed out at that point and stayed in the garden until I went out with her coat and hat in my hand just a while before we left. I can sense her still sulking as she drags along behind me. But as we reach the station entrance, any thoughts of Jessica's sullen mood vanish. A crowd of what appears to be hundreds of Tamarisk Bay folk – mostly women – are standing in and around the station forecourt, shuffling to find space. This is no mother's meeting, no joyous organisation of folk planning the next Harvest Festival. As I glance around, I see many faces I recognise, each one tight with apprehension. Some nod at me as I catch their eye. Some are grasping the hands of their children, a few are accompanied by their husband. I'm irritated that George isn't here beside me, from the moment we have to choose a vulnerable child, taking him or her by the hand. Because they will be vulnerable, every last one of them, of that I'm certain.

I scour the crowd and spot Ronnie's mum, Clara, in the distance. She raises a hand to wave, but there are too many people between us for me to get any closer so that we can talk. We've been friends for years, since before Philip was born. It would be reassuring to stand beside her while we wait. Some kind of strength in numbers, which would sound ridiculous if I said such a thing out loud. It's the children who will step off the train who will need reassuring.

Standing away from the throng is Mr Cowdry. He's something with the Council, I think. He's standing behind a big chalk board. 'Billeting Office this way' is written large across it, with an arrow pointing to the gate that takes you outside the station concourse and up to the village hall. It looks as though some of the women are lining up to speak to him, perhaps to find out more about how this is all going to work. We haven't been given names or details of which child might be placed with us. No one has even asked us how many we can take.

We've been told the train is due in at half-past twelve, but beyond that we know very little about any arrangements. I guess the children and any adults who have travelled with them will be taken to the Billeting Office and there'll be paperwork to complete.

'You're Philip's mum, aren't you?' The woman's face is familiar, but I can't place her.

'Me and my husband have Marley's butcher's down Court Street,. Young Ronnie has not long since started working for us. The number of times I've seen your Philip hanging around outside the shop waiting for Ronnie to finish, I'm guessing they must be bosom pals.'

'Of course, Mrs Marley. I'm so used to seeing you in the shop, I didn't recognise you without your butcher's apron.' I smile and hold out my hand to shake hers.

'Planning to take one of these poor mites, are you?' She nods towards the empty train track. 'I can't imagine what it must be like for them, leaving their families, travelling all that way. I wouldn't be surprised if some of them have never even see the sea, or a cow in a field, come to that.' She laughs and then continues. 'I was brought up in a city so I can speak from experience. I was fourteen years old when I first saw the sea and I was terrified of it. Certain that eerie monsters would crawl out of the water and up the shingle to get me.' She laughs again, a hearty laugh that leads me to smile. 'I expect your Philip misses his pal on a Saturday morning, but it's our busy time so we can't spare Ronnie. Or does your lad have a job now?'

It's only now I realise I've lost sight of Philip and Jessica. Then Mr Cowdry calls out, 'Can I have your attention please.' People nudge each other, some asking for hush while others continue to chatter, but a little quieter than before.

'The train will arrive shortly. I will lead the children from the platform down to the village hall and if you can all follow.'

'How long's it going to take?' one woman shouts out. 'I've left a steam pudding on the stove and if I don't get back soon the saucepan will burn dry.'

'More fool you,' another calls out, while a snigger goes through the crowd.

'It will take as long as it takes,' Mr Cowdry says, and with that comes the sound of the train entering the station.

I am certain that the scenes I see over the next twenty minutes or so will remain with me forever. The train doors open, releasing hundreds of children, that spill onto the platform like sacks of mail. Short and tall, the smallest clinging tightly to the hands of older ones. Many with faces smeared with tears as well as grime, others eager and bright-eyed, elbowing their way to the front. Each child has their gas mask slung across one shoulder and a label pinned to their coats. As some walk past me I read a few of the labels that merely show their name, home address and destination – Tamarisk Bay - each child a little parcel sent by a loving parent to an unknown recipient. Most carry a small case or satchel, with barely space for one or two things, certainly not all their belongings.

My focus lands on one little girl, her blonde pigtails swinging back and forth as she walks. She carries a teddy bear, held tight to her chest as if she is determined to protect it from any and all threats. An older boy – her brother, perhaps – puts his hand on her shoulder, guiding her along the platform towards the exit. His expression is fixed, resilient, as if he alone has been handed a responsibility that surely weighs too heavy on a child who can be little more than ten or eleven.

Again, my thoughts go to my own children. I scan the crowd and see Jessica several feet away, arm in arm with Lucy, both of them chattering, oblivious to all that is happening around them. Philip is nowhere to be seen.

'Jessica,' I call out across the platform. Several of the new arrivals look up. I call again, but it's only on the third occasion that I gain the attention of my daughter. I beckon her towards me and after a few minutes she ambles over.

'Where's Philip? Have you seen him?' I ask her, knowing even as I say it that it's a wasted question. Her response is a shrug.

'Stay beside me now, Jessica. We need to follow the children into the village hall. It's important that you don't wander off again. Do you understand? Philip will just have to find us, we can't wait for him.'

'But I want to play with Lucy. Why do we have to go to the village hall? It's boring.'

'All these children have to find new families to live with. I'm sure they'd like to be home playing with their best friends too, instead they've left all that behind and now we need to be kind to them and look after them.'

'If they touch any of my things they'll be in trouble.'

I choose not to respond.

Once inside the village hall, the noise is such that it is almost impossible to hear anything Mr Cowdry is attempting to say. I catch the odd word, but nothing that tells me what might happen next. The evacuees appear as mystified as the adults. It seems there has been little if any planning as to how the placement of the children should be organised. I watch as one woman steps forward and leans down to speak to two boys who are standing to one side of the rest. They are of similar height and build, twins perhaps? She guides the boys to the front of the hall where two women are sitting at a table and appearing to be taking instructions from Mr Cowdry. There is a brief conversation, some details entered into some kind of register that sits on the table in front of them and the woman and the two boys leave the hall. Clearly, I haven't been the only one watching this transaction as over the next ten minutes other women step forward, approaching one or more of the children, taking them up to Mr Cowdry's assistants, before leaving with their new charges.

Now Mr Cowdry claps his hands to gain everyone's attention. 'Children, the kind people of Tamarisk Bay are prepared to take you into their homes and families. So, if you can come up onto the stage please. Line up and look straight ahead, no pushing or shoving and no talking.'

The evacuees are guided up the few steps onto the stage, the little ones being pulled along by the older ones. Most of them look petrified, their fears made worse when Mr Cowdry walks along the line as if inspecting an army brigade.

'Now ladies,' he says. 'If you can make your choice. Form an orderly queue, come up onto the stage, choose your child or children, and give your details to Mrs Spencer or Mrs White. Name, address and who it is you've taken. There will be more paperwork to fill in at a later date, but for now we just need to clear the hall as quickly as possible.'

On the far side of the hall is another table filled with jugs of lemonade and plates of arrowroot biscuits. God alone knows how long it has been since any of the children have had their breakfast. I ease my way to the front of the hall and tap Mr Cowdry on the arm.

'It might be an idea to let the children have a drink and a biscuit first, don't you think?' I say, loudly enough that his helpers can hear.

'Yes, yes, of course,' one of the helpers says. 'Bill, I know we have a lot to get through, but it won't hurt for the children to have five minutes for some refreshment.'

Bill Cowdry mutters something under his breath. It seems his makeshift army corporals are verging on a mutiny. I cross over to the refreshments table, pour lemonade into several glasses, putting them onto a tray, together with a plate loaded with biscuits.

'Jessica, you can help. Follow me up onto the stage and help the children to take a drink and a biscuit, will you?'

My daughter's expression is a picture. A mix of indignation and pride; a chance to stand out from the crowd, even though it means acting as a waitress to a bunch of children who threaten to interfere with all she has known to date.

Two other women follow my lead as we move up and down the line of the children. As I reach the last child, standing at the far side of the stage, I offer up the tray to him.

'You must be thirsty, help yourself to a biscuit too,' I say.

He is gazing down at the floor so I can't see his face, just the top of his head. There is barely any hair left after what must have been a severe haircut in preparation for the journey. He has outgrown his raincoat, which is tight across his shoulders, patched in several places on the sleeves, the belt pulled around his middle. Around his neck a woollen scarf. I follow his focus and notice he is wearing wellington boots, the front of the left one revealing a gap between the sole and the upper. His hands are stuffed in the pockets of his raincoat and the kit bag that must contain all his belongings hangs off him on one side, the case with his gas mask on the other.

'What's your name, son?' I ask him. His label is either hidden by the collar of his raincoat, or it has fallen off.

'Answer the lady, boy.' Only as he speaks do I notice that Mr Cowdry is standing beside me. He puts a hand on the boy's shoulder, but the boy pulls away and as he does he looks up at me, a defiant stare. 'Hasn't anyone taught you manners, boy.' Mr Cowdry continues.

'It's alright, Mr Cowdry. The lad has had a distressing time of it. All the children have. Let's not make things worse by shouting.'

Now it is Mr Cowdry who stares at me. Not defiance, but disgust. I have a fleeting thought about what George might say if he was here. Jessica has wandered off, seemingly bored with playing the role of waitress, and Philip has yet to turn up.

A few moments later, Mr Cowdry is back on the main floor of the hall, moving among the adults, exchanging a few words with one or two. Then he walks back to the stage and calls for quiet.

'Now that refreshments have been enjoyed, it's time to get on with the principal business of the day. If each of you could come up and choose your child. Children, when you are asked a question, please reply politely. You're in Tamarisk Bay now and in this town children behave themselves and respect their elders.'

Over the next half hour there is a continual flow of adults being paired up with children. 'I'll take that one,' I hear repeated over and over and each time I hear it my spirits sink a little lower. All well intended, I'm sure, but there must be a better way.

Gradually, the number of children remaining on the stage dwindles to a handful. The boy I spoke to earlier is now sitting cross-legged on the floor, his shoulders slumped forward as he runs his fingers through the dust. As I go back up onto the stage to speak to him, Philip comes into the hall. I see him searching for me among the crowd, and I hold up my hand to get his attention.

'Mum, sorry. I got chatting with some friends and then I didn't know where you were. Where's Jess?'

'You know Jessica, never keen on doing what she's asked.' I pull my son to one side and lower my voice. 'Philip, will you come over and speak to that lad with me. I think maybe he's shy, but you're closer in age to him, he might open up to you.'

My son nods and follows me to stand beside the boy. Philip crouches down and sits cross-legged, mirroring the boy's position.

'Are you any good at climbing trees?' Philip says.

He has taken the boy by surprise. He stops running his fingers through the dust and looks up, first at Philip, then at me.

'I can tell you're taller than me, even though you're sitting down. My legs are too short, so I'm rubbish at it. I can never get up high enough to get the best views, or the best apples.'

'Don't know,' the boy says.

'Well, I reckon you'd be good and if you fancy giving it a go I can take you to the very best place for scrumping.' Philip avoids my gaze, as we both know he would be in trouble if he was ever caught stealing apples. But I let it go. The important thing right now is to gain the boy's trust and if that means I didn't hear what my son just suggested, it's a small price to pay.

'I'm Philip, by the way,' my son continues.

'Charlie,' the boy says, reverting to a downward gaze.

'Nice to meet you, Charlie,' Philip says. 'Do you fancy it? We could go over there this afternoon if you like.'

'What's scrumping?' Charlie says.

THREE

GEORGE

I CONTINUE DIGGING THE back garden while Helen is out collecting the newcomer to our family. I'd already cut away the greater part of the back lawn last weekend to create the chicken run. Now it's the turn of the flower borders. As I push the fork into the soil and pull out the dahlia tubers that are still in flower, I'm reminded of the summer when Helen first planted them. For weeks after she took to gazing from the kitchen window as if willing them to bloom.

It's moments like those that take me back to our courting days. I'd arrive at her family home, clutching a single flower, grabbed from my father's garden and often getting a clip round the ear if he caught me. I always reckoned the flower acted as a passport, allowing my entry into Helen's home, her family, and ultimately, her heart. Although whenever I remind her of all that she says nothing, leaving me thinking the memories are only mine.

With war on the horizon, we need to hunker down. The area for the chickens is already well established; five chickens each contributing an egg a day. And now, in place of dahlias and lawn, we will have potatoes, onions and carrots so that my family will at least have soups and vegetable stews to see them through the winter. I won't be here, but knowing my children will be well fed is a comfort of sorts.

Thinking about the work needed to keep on top of the vegetable plot, I'm hoping Helen will bring a boy back with her. A sturdy pair of hands to share the heavy chores with Philip.

I don't hear them arrive. Only when I stop for a glass of water, do I find them all in the kitchen.

'Welcome to the Chandler family, lad. What's your name?'

The boy is standing in the far corner of the kitchen, close to the doorway, as if hoping to make a quick getaway. He looks younger than Philip, yet is just as tall as him, if not taller. He is holding what looks like a sack or kit bag in front of him, close to his chest, as if it contains precious jewels.

'This is Charlie,' Helen says. 'I'll get us all something to eat. Looks as though you've been busy.' She nods towards the kitchen window, where the garden landscape is nothing more than uneven banks of soil, either side of muddy trenches.

'There's a lot more to do yet. Maybe Philip and Charlie can help me this afternoon.' I direct my words at the evacuee. I have yet to get a proper look at his face.

'Let the lad settle first. It hasn't been an easy morning for him.' Helen gives me a warning glance. 'Philip, why don't you could take Charlie up to your bedroom and make some space in the chest of drawers for his things. Jessica, lay the table will you? I'm going to see what your dad's been doing in the back garden.' Helen gestures to me to follow her.

'It was dreadful, George, really dreadful,' she says once we are both outside. 'Mr Cowdry was there, lording it over the whole thing. I'm sure he thought those poor children were nothing more than a load of conscripts in his own private army.'

'It can't have been easy for him. These things have to be managed or they can turn into chaos.'

She glares at me.

'What made you choose Charlie?' I ask her. 'He seems like a sullen lad.' I'm unlikely to soften her mood, nevertheless I continue. 'What do you know about him? What sort of family does it come from?'

'I need to get lunch ready,' is her only reply.

'His father might be a farmer. He could turn out to be just what we need,' I say, touching her arm for a moment before she walks away.

'I doubt it. He's never even climbed a tree.'

And with that she's gone and I'm left wondering how the coming days and weeks will be.

Lunch is an awkward, silent affair, a stark contrast to our usual family mealtime chatter. I find myself grateful I'll soon be rejoining my regiment and then instantly guilty at having such thoughts.

Leaving Jessica to help Helen clear away the lunch things, I return to my digging. There's a satisfaction in the physical motion of forcing the spade into the earth, breaking up the solid clumps of soil, the sweat running down my back. All week I sit in a stuffy office, shuffling papers, totting up columns of figures. Same job, same office since I first started work, with the only break being my years at the front in the Great War. Many would call me lucky to still be in work, particularly all those men who lost their job during the depression.

And that's what Helen reminds me of each Friday, when I put my wages on the kitchen table. 'At least you've got a job,' she tells me as she divides up the pounds and shillings, some for food, some for rent. Some into the empty Brooke Bond tea tin for coal and electricity, and some set aside for the children's clothes. The little that's left over she gives back to me. 'Beer money,' she tells me. It's rare for me to go to the pub, nevertheless I take the money. It's been years since Helen bought herself a new dress, so that's my plan. The unspent beer money will eventually mean my wife can choose a whole new outfit. I intend to tell her about it before I leave for the front, but I can guess at her response. 'What do I need a new outfit for?' It's true she's unlikely to be going out anywhere fancy with a war just around the corner, but just knowing she has something new and pretty will make me feel better about leaving her. 'You can wear it when I come home,' I'll tell her, knowing the doubts we share about when or if I'll see her again. Doubts that remain unspoken.

Whenever Helen reminds me how lucky I am to still be in work, I know I should be honest and tell her how much I hate my job. I always have. As I continue to dig and churn the soil, I make myself a promise. When I return from this war, I'll take the leap, make a change. I've always fancied being a ship's captain, although all I know about the sea is the changing of the tides. Perhaps I should have asked to join the navy. At least I'd have learned a little about how to steer a ship into harbour, how to drop anchor and suchlike. But back then they needed foot soldiers, 'cannon fodder' some called us. And for the thousands who never returned I guess that's what they were.

FOUR

HELEN

Sunday is usually our quiet day, our family day. But this Sunday will be the first of something different. We need to find a new way of being. Instead the days starts with division.

At breakfast Jessica sits opposite Charlie at the breakfast table, glaring at him in-between working through a bowl of cornflakes.

'Will you have cornflakes too, Charlie?' I ask him. The packet is on the table, as is the jug of milk and bowl of sugar, but his bowl is empty. As he stretches his hand across to take the cereal packet, Jessica takes the other side of it. But any minor tug of war is short-lived as Charlie drops his hand.

'Jessica, I'll not tell you again. Have you forgotten all your manners?' I say.

As she lets go of the packet I take it, shaking cornflakes into Charlie's bowl. 'Milk? Sugar?' I ask him. 'What do you usually have for breakfast? Would you like a slice of bread and jam instead?'

Once more a shrug is his only response. But at least he starts to eat the cornflakes, albeit dry, without either milk or sugar.

Straight after breakfast George heads out to the back garden continuing his project to transform my garden into a mud patch. I know the way those words sound as I say them in my head, as if my husband is to blame for all that is happening around us and of course, that's just not true. He is as much a victim as the rest of us.

Philip offers to take Charlie out to meet up with Ronnie, and as there is no spare bike for Charlie it means having to forego their usual Sunday morning bike ride.

'We'll go to the woods, I'll show you the very best trees to climb.' I hear the forced jollity in Philip's voice that I'd heard in my own just yesterday. 'You'll like Ronnie,' he continued. 'He's good fun. He's older than me, but we've been friends since forever.'

I watch Philip's expression as he pauses.

'I expect you miss your friends,' he continues.

Charlie has yet to say more than a few words and despite George wanting me to push the lad for answers to questions about his life in London, I'm sure that persistent badgering will make him close up even more.

'He'll tell us in his own good time,' I tell George. 'And even if he doesn't what does it matter? Let him settle. I'll leave it a few days then maybe suggest he writes a letter to his folks, reassure them he's being looked after.'

After clearing away the breakfast things I begin to prepare Sunday lunch. Each time I call out to Jessica to help me she tells me she is 'too busy'. When she emerges, it is with dust and cobwebs in her hair.

'What have you been doing?' I ask her.

'I'm sorting out the box room to make space for a bed,' is her defiant reply.

I don't have the energy or desire to argue with her.

A church service is just ending on the wireless. It's followed by band music with such a lively tone it feels entirely inappropriate. I find myself irritated with the people who choose such programmes, surely they must understand that people across the land are feeling anything but lively.

Just as the presenter introduces the next piece, I decide to do something that feels furtive and dishonest. First I check that George is still engrossed in his digging. Then I go upstairs. Once on the landing I listen out for Jessica, hoping she will not choose this moment to emerge from her dusty 'tidying' of the box room. I creep along the landing as quietly as I can and ease open Philip's bedroom door.

Both beds are still unmade, so I spend a few moments tidying the covers, smoothing out the bedspreads. We've made a makeshift bed for Charlie from some old sofa cushions. It's not ideal, but until we can lay our hands on a second-hand bed, it will have to do. There are a few dirty clothes in a pile at the bottom of Philip's bed, which will go into Monday's wash, and as I check through them I'm reminded how worn all his shirts are. I make a mental note to add them to my mending pile. By turning the collars they'll last him a while yet.

Now to my real reason for venturing into my son's bedroom. I slide open the top drawer of the chest, the one I suggested Philip offered to Charlie. I'm not sure what I'm expecting to find, even so, seeing the drawer nearly empty is a surprise. There's a brown paper bag containing a toothbrush, a small pat of soap and a comb. The only other item is a little wooden boat. I pick it up, careful not to damage it as parts of it appear fragile. It's clearly been hand made, carved from a piece of oak. The wheel is fixed securely on a little wooden post, as is the rear propeller. There is even a front screen, made from a piece of netting, something to protect the imaginary sailor from the worst of turbulent waves. This has been made with care and love. Across the side of the bow are hand-painted letters: 'C E M'. Below the letters this little boat carries a brave and strong name: 'HMS Beagle'. The name of Charles Darwin's ship that took him around the world for five years, during which time he developed his theory of evolution. For a moment I'm lost in thoughts of Darwin, what he might think if he returned to the world now, to see how mankind has evolved, turning our backs on peace and harmony, choosing destruction instead.

A noise out on the landing brings me back to the moment. I return the boat to the drawer and glance around the room for Charlie's other belongings. Surely he must have brought some clothes, a change of underwear, socks, shirt? The kit bag he was clinging on to when he arrived is now hooked over the back of a chair, together with the old raincoat he had outgrown a long time past. As soon as I lift the kit bag, I can tell it is empty, nevertheless I pull open the string and put my hand inside. One item remains at the bottom of the bag. As I take it out I see it is a small photograph. A man, his face weathered, a flat cap on his head, his shirt open, sleeves rolled up, braces over broad shoulders. Everything about the man and his surroundings are rough and tough, yet on his face is a broad smile, as if the person wielding the camera had told him the very best of jokes. Charlie's father, perhaps? I wonder why the photo hasn't gone into the drawer, or better still under his pillow.

But now the footsteps outside the door tells me that Jessica has emerged from the box room. I return the photo to its original place and hook the kit bag back onto the chair. As I step outside the bedroom Jessica is standing in front of me.

'Will you help me, mummy?' she says. 'I really, really want to have my own bedroom. I don't even mind about not having a window.' She turns her face to gaze at me and as she does I feel a sinking desperation.

'We'll do what we can, darling. But I'm making no promises.'

As I return to the kitchen, the wireless is no longer playing music. Instead I hear the Prime Minister's voice. I bang hard on the window, trying to grab George's attention. I don't want to leave the broadcast to fetch him. And then I hear Chamberlain uttering the words we knew were coming, but ones we prayed we would never hear. Our country is at war. Again.

FIVE

GEORGE

Yesterday's announcement was not unexpected, nevertheless it's confirmation that my plans are the right plans. This morning I will tell Mr Williams that I'll leave at the end of next week. There'll be a period of retraining, of course, and then I'll go wherever I'm needed. I don't have any particular skills. Men working for haulage firms can use their driving experience to man goods vehicles, transporting vital supplies. Quantity surveyors are experts in plotting and planning, making them perfect for the tricky job of navigating for air crew. I'm good with numbers, but that was something that made little or no difference in the Great War. That wasn't a war fought with brains or tactics, it was a brutal war, relying on face-to-face combat between the young generations of countries who had no choice but to make the ultimate sacrifice. Right now it's impossible to imagine what kind of brutality we will see this time around. All we can hope for is that lessons have been learned, otherwise what was the point of it all.

By the time I sit for breakfast, Philip has already left for work at the sorting office. He has to be there for six each morning. I'm planning to leave earlier than usual as I can sense there will be an argument if Helen attempts to persuade Jessica to accompany Charlie to school. I'm in no mood for confrontation, there'll be enough of that soon enough.

'You won't be the only new boy,' I hear Helen say to Charlie as I fetch my jacket from the hallway. Her voice is overly cheery, suggesting a mood I'm certain she isn't feeling. 'You might even find you have friends from home in your new class.'

I call out, 'Goodbye', grateful to avoid the rest of the conversation, and vaguely wondering how it will be resolved.

Once I'm in the office all the talk is about Chamberlain's announcement. We are a team of five book-keepers, the others all younger than me.

'They'll want the youngsters first, though, won't they?' Fred Soames says. I can't help noticing more than a little wistfulness in his tone. 'Best to wait until we're contacted. What are you going to do, George? They won't expect you to fight again, will they?'

Perhaps he's right. Volunteers will be needed to join the existing Air Raid Precautions workers, knocking on doors to warn people their blackout curtains aren't quite doing the job, or guiding people to air-raid shelters. But doesn't my weapons experience count for anything? I can handle a Lee Enfield rifle, I'm familiar with its bolt action, the importance of reloading it quickly, efficiently. I've worked with machine guns too.

'I'm planning to rejoin my regiment,' I tell Fred. 'I guess Mr Williams will need to employ new staff to replace us. We'll all be needed in the end.'

Fred's response is a raised eyebrow.

I wait until later in the day to request an appointment with Mr Williams. Most of the day he sits inside his office with the door closed, only emerging on occasion to walk past our desks, like a schoolmaster checking on his pupils. Mid-afternoon he ventures past my desk and I grab my chance.

'Mr Williams, could I have a word?'

Alfred Williams has only been with the firm for the last five years or so. He took over the role of Managing Director when his father passed away. Old Mr Williams was a kindly soul, focused on the wellbeing of the firm, of course, but also concerned for the wellbeing of his staff. On Monday mornings he would regularly come out into the main office, pull up a chair and spend a few minutes just chatting. He'd share an anecdote or two about his weekend and encourage us to do the same. But once his son took over, the Monday morning chats became a thing of the past. Now, the sole focus is efficiency and productivity.

'Is it important?' Alfred Williams says, slowing his pace to stand in front of my desk.

'Er, yes, sir.' I stutter a little, running through the justification in my mind. Not a justification that I need to join the fighting, merely that I want a few moments of my boss's time. Has it really come to that?

'Four thirty,' he says, then turns and re-enters his office, closing the door behind him.

'He can't stop you, you know. If that's what you're worried about,' Fred says in a low voice. 'Like you said, every one of us will have to go at some point. Good for you, I say. What do you think, Bernard? You'll be gone soon too, won't you?'

Bernard Lancing has most recently joined us. He can't be more than twenty-two. He may even be younger, his face looks as though it rarely needs shaving, just like my Philip.

'Mum doesn't want me to go. She says I could be one of those conscientious objectors, tell them I'd don't agree with fighting. Well, I don't, not really.' Bernard looks as me as if seeking reassurance.

'You don't want to go down that road,' I tell him. 'You could end up going to prison. Then what would your mother do?'

'At least he'll be alive,' Fred says, returning to the papers on his desk, signalling an end to the conversation.

At four-thirty I knock on Mr Williams' door. A few moments pass before he calls out, 'Enter'.

As I push the door open it's the smell of pipe smoke that reaches me first, then the taste of it. It's so thick it creates a haze, blurring the image of Mr Williams, who is sitting at his large oak desk, his hands laid flat on the blotter. He appears to be studying his fingernails.

'Mr Chandler. Yes, you wanted a word?' He is speaking to me, but he remains distracted. Then he says, 'Do you know, Mr Chandler, these hands have killed a man. What do you think to that, eh?'

He looks up, but not at me, rather through me, at some memory he is revisiting.

'The Great War?' I ask him.

'Thought that was the end of it, didn't we? Well, we got that wrong.'

'I intend to rejoin my regiment, Mr Williams. That's what I wanted to tell you.'

Now he is gazing directly at me, studying my face, his eyes scanning me. 'And you think they'll want you, do you? How old are you, Mr Chandler?'

'Forty-one, Sir.'

'Well I can tell you now that they won't want you. In fact, I'll go as far as to say that they'll laugh at your suggestion and send you home. You have a family?'

'Yes, Sir.'

'Look to your family, Mr Chandler. That's my advice to you.' He stands, pushing the chair away from his desk and moves to gaze out of the window, turning his back on me. 'Well, if that's all, you'd best get back to your work. We don't finish until five, so there's plenty still to be done.'

I sidle out of his office, returning to my desk, avoiding the questioning glances from my colleagues.

At five I tidy the papers I've been working on, putting everything into my desk drawer. By five-thirty I am home. I go in the front door, hang my jacket on the coat stand, and before I can exchange my shoes for slippers Helen is standing in front of me holding the Brooke Bond tea tin. She pushes it into my hands.

'Open it. Go on, open it. It's all gone, George. Every last penny.'

I take the tin from her and do as she asks. The tin is empty.

'Oh, George, what are we going to do? The coal man is due tomorrow. He'll need paying and we'll need money for the electricity meter. If it's not enough that the Nazis want to invade us, now we've got to protect ourselves from burglars coming into our house. It's too much, George.'

She cups her face in her hands, then turns away from me before I can say a word. I follow her into the kitchen, where she drops onto a chair, looking up at me like a bewildered puppy.

'Steady on there, darling. There'll be an explanation, I'm sure of it. When did you first notice the money was gone?'

'I'd been out in the garden, raking over the soil. I came in to get tea ready for everyone and the empty tin was on the table. It's not as if the burglar has even tried to disguise the theft. Brazen it is. Just leaving it there for me to find.'

'And you didn't see anyone? While you were out in the garden? No one going along the back path?'

She shakes her head. 'We'll have to tell the police. For all we know someone is helping themselves to whatever they can find, working their way along the whole street.' Her voice raises to a pitch.

'Let's calm down, shall we? Where are Charlie and Jessica? Maybe they saw something. Were they home at the usual time from school?'

Before she can answer the back door opens and Philip comes in, kicking off his shoes and going straight to the sink to fill a glass of water.

'Crikey, what a day,' he says. 'The bosses are panicking that all the postmen will want to leave to enlist. I reckon they'll be wanting me to do longer hours, which means a few more pounds every week, so that should help...' He pauses as he notices his mother peering into the empty tea tin as though a magic trick had been performed in front of her and she is struggling to see how it has been achieved. 'Mum? Is there a problem?'

'We've been burgled,' Helen says, slamming the tin down on the table, startling both Philip and me.

'Have you called the police?' Philip asks.

Before either of us can answer Jessica dances into the kitchen, her pigtails swinging, her face flushed from running.

'Where's Charlie?' I ask her.

'I took him to the woods, then I met up with Lucy and I thought he'd probably come back home. Isn't he here?'

Helen and I exchange a look, which doesn't go unnoticed by Philip.

'Let's find Charlie first, shall we?' I say.

SIX

HELEN

GEORGE DOESN'T HAVE TO say what we are both thinking. We know nothing about Charlie, except that he has been thrown into a new life with strangers. A life he hasn't chosen. And yet as I have the unspoken thoughts that I know will lead us to accusations, I feel a burden of guilt. I have already failed this young boy who has been entrusted to our care. But it is guilt underpinned with anger. Money is tight, and yet we have always made sure we didn't go into debt. Unless I can retrieve the money from Charlie, we will owe money that we won't be able to pay.

'Jessica, take me to where you left Charlie. In the woods, you said?'

'But I haven't had my tea,' Jessica says, sitting at the kitchen table with a look of expectation.

'Jessica,' George says. 'Do as your mother says. There will be no tea until we have found Charlie.'

Jessica grumbles something, which I don't catch.

'Shall I come too, Mum?' Philip asks.

'No, you stay here with your dad. Charlie might come straight back here and if he does...well, perhaps he'll talk to you, we need to try to understand why he's done what he's done.'

'You think Charlie has stolen the tea tin money?' Philip says, directing his question at George.

'We just need to find him and then everything will become clear,' George replies.

I have my doubts that anything will be clear, not today and not for a long time yet, but I stay quiet, take Jessica's hand and head out the front door.

'He said he wanted to climb those trees again,' Jessica says as we head towards the woods. 'The ones that Philip and Ronnie showed him and the ones Philip never lets me climb. It's not fair, Charlie is nearly the same age as me. How come he can climb trees and I can't?'

Jessica tugs her hand away from me and it's only then I'm aware that I've been pulling her in my haste to reach the woods.

'Sorry, Jessica, but this isn't the time for dawdling.'

'My legs won't move as quickly as yours.'

'Your legs move quickly enough when you're off running and playing with Lucy.' My tone is sharp, which I regret as soon as the words leave my lips. The predicament we find ourselves in is not my daughter's fault.

As soon as we reach the wooded area where the children usually play there is no sign of Charlie. I call his name a few times in the vain hope he might appear from behind a clump of trees.

'And you left him here?' I ask my daughter.

'Yes, he climbed up one of the trees and I got bored waiting for him to come down. Lucy's mum has made her a new skirt, she told me about it when we were at school today and I wanted to see it.'

'It wasn't very kind of you, Jessica. Just leaving Charlie like that. He hasn't had a chance to find his way around Tamarisk Bay yet, so he may not be able to find his way home.'

'To London?'

'Charlie's home is with us for now. It might be a long time before he can go back to his real home, back to London.'

She walks ahead of me, suddenly putting on a pace that requires me to run a few steps to catch her up. We come out into the clearing that leads us in turn back onto Archery Road. I'm wondering which direction to take next when I spot Deirdre White walking towards me on the opposite pavement. She lifts a hand to wave and I cross the road.

'Out for a nice walk with your mum, are you, Jessica?' Deirdre says.

'We're just trying to catch up with Charlie. The young evacuee who joined us on Saturday,' I say, as if the phrases are the most natural thing in the world to be saying. 'I don't suppose you've seen him, have you? He's about this height.' I position my hand about a foot above Jessica's head.

'Raincoat about three sizes too small?' Deirdre says.

I nod, feeling a churning in the pit of my stomach.

'Poor mites, aren't they? Good of you to take one, though. We've all got to do our bit, haven't we? We've got two of them. Brother and sister. Sweet as anything, but the pair of them spent the first evening crying. It's no surprise, is it? But right now we're all they've got. And we're the lucky ones, aren't we? Goodness only knows what their parents are going through.'

'Where did you see him?' I ask her.

'Down by the fishing huts. Chatting to old Bill Marchant.'

I won't allow my fears to show on my face. I grab Jessica's hand again, thank Deirdre and move on quickly down London Road onto the seafront and on towards the Old Town. What would have drawn Charlie to stray so far from our house? I am reminded of a conversation I had with Mrs Marley on the day we first met the evacuees. We reflected on what it must be like for city children to see the coast for the first time. Of course, Charlie would be attracted towards the beach. I'm annoyed with myself for not thinking about it before now. We could have taken him there yesterday, gone as a family, as we have done so many times before. And yet yesterday we weren't a family, we were divided, fault lines appearing in what used to be solid ground.

As we make our way along the seafront towards the Old Town harbour, I scour the faces of each person we pass. There are few people out at this time of day, folk enjoying their tea and settling indoors before the fading evening light means the blackout curtains must be drawn. This war is making prisoners of us all.

And then, I see him, in the distance. He is standing beside Mr Marchant, engaged in conversation. A boy who has hardly spoken more than a dozen words since he arrived with us on Saturday, is now comfortably chatting with a stranger.

I let go of Jessica's hand in my haste to reach Charlie, leaving her to follow me onto the beach. As I get closer to Charlie he turns away from me and moves towards one of the fishing boats that has been pulled up onto the shingle. Soon the fishermen will no longer be able to ply their trade, the younger ones will enlist, leaving the older ones to risk enemy fire if their boats are spotted out in the Channel.

'Charlie.' I call out to him. Then again, this time a little louder. 'Charlie.'

He remains some distance away, still with his back to me. Instead it is Mr Marchant who approaches.

'Mrs Chandler, isn't it?'

I'm surprised he knows my name.

'The lad's as bright as a button, isn't he?' Mr Marchant says.

I stand a little way off from Mr Marchant, with Jessica now beside me.

'Is he?' I ask, feeling foolish in part, but also uncomfortable with the thought of my young charge spending time with a man I know little about. We don't listen to rumours, George had said just days ago. But don't people also say, 'there's no smoke without fire.'

'I'm afraid Charlie has done a terrible thing, Mr Marchant, and that's what I need to speak to him about.'

'Bad thing, you say?'

'Yes.'

'He doesn't strike me as a bad'un. If my Jack had had a son he would have been just the same age as young Charlie here. A grandson he'd be. Now there's a thought – a grand son.' He looks into the distance, his expression pensive, one hand stroking his wispy white beard.

'Your son, Jack?' I repeat the name, not focusing on any possible reply.

'He was killed in the Somme, like so many young men. Doesn't seem right, does it? The young ones being taken like that; a whole generation.'

'I'm so sorry, Mr Marchant, but I really need to talk to Charlie now and I need to get him and Jessica home. My husband will be worried.'

'Martha never got over it. Losing Jack. Our only child, and such a brilliant fisherman as a lad. Sounds like your Charlie might go the same way, given half the chance.'

'He's not my Charlie... sorry, Mr Marchant did you say that Charlie knows how to fish?'

'Not fishing so much. It's ships he knows about. Great things, bigger than anything you see going in and out of Tidehaven. His dad works on the docks. It'll be down to the likes of Charlie's dad to see us through the war, you see if it's not.'

I leave Bill Marchant behind me. He is still talking, but his voice fading as I walk towards Charlie. I put my hand on his shoulder, he resists a little, then turns to face me.

'It's time to go, Charlie. You'll be hungry, I expect.'

On our journey home I attempt to engage Charlie in conversation, but the 'bright lad' who opened himself up to Bill Marchant has now retreated behind his protective shell. With Jessica in earshot, this is not the time to ask him about the money he has stolen; better to tackle that subject with George and I posing the questions. As we walk the last stretch in silence, I consider my approach. A direct accusation is bound to get us nowhere, just as likely he will take off, leaving us searching for him once again.

'Jessica, you're dawdling.' She is some way behind us, appearing to be playing an imaginary game that involves not stepping on the lines in the pavement.

'I'm hungry,' is her only reply.

We have reached the house. George is in the front garden, leaning on the gate. As soon as he catches sight of us turning the corner he comes out into the street, walking up to meet us.

'You found him,' he says. 'Where?'

I shake my head. 'Let's get inside. The children are hungry.'

The table is laid, a loaf ready on the bread board, butter in the dish, a slab of cheese and a bowl of apples completing the offering.

'You waited,' I say, although I expected nothing else.

Philip is staring at Charlie and I sense he is about to launch into accusations. But then Charlie surprises us all.

'That man I met. Down by the fishing boats.'

It feels as though we are all holding our breath.

'He reminds me of my granddad,' he continues. 'I miss him and I miss my dad. When can I go home?'

Any anger I had when I discovered my empty money tin vanishes. A wave of sadness washes over me.

'We don't know the answer to that, Charlie. None of us know what's going to happen. How about you write a letter to your dad? Maybe tell him you met Mr Marchant. Sounds like you had a good chat to him. And your dad works at the docks?'

There is a moment when I'm certain Charlie is ready to open up, but the moment passes when George coughs, and gestures to me.

'Mrs Chandler and I need to talk to you, Charlie,' he says. 'Jessica, Philip, sit down and start your tea. Your mother and I are going to talk to Charlie in the other room and then we'll be back.'

George points at the door and steps forward. I want to stop this. I want us all to sit at the table together, to make Charlie feel a part of our family, to encourage him to tell us about his own family and only then will we be able to understand why he felt he needed to steal from us. But that opportunity has passed.

SEVEN

George

I'm relieved when I see them turn the corner into our road. All the while that Helen has been off searching for Charlie, Philip has been pestering me.

'What will you do, Dad? Will you have to tell the police about Charlie? What will happen to him?'

I avoid all his questions, not because I don't want to answer him, but because I can't. The boy has done wrong and will need to be punished. All we can hope for is that he still has the money in his pocket. At the very least, that will be a positive result.

As soon as I see them walking towards me I can tell from Helen's demeanour that she has mellowed. Her fury has vanished. It must be something to do with being a mother. And when Charlie begins to tell us of his family in London, I can tell that her priorities have changed. She has forgotten the desperation of not being able to pay the bills, she feels sorry for the lad. Now it is me who is filled with fury. We have taken Charlie into our home and this is how he chooses to repay us.

Helen and Charlie shuffle in behind me and I close the sitting-room door.

'Charlie,' I start, ignoring Helen's warning glance. 'We know you stole money from the tin and we need you to give it back. That money is for paying bills.'

Charlie looks at me as if I am speaking a strange language.

'Charlie, do you understand what I'm saying? Do you still have the money?'

He fixes his gaze on me, but is silent.

'If you give it all back, we won't have to involve the police. But you need to understand that this is a very serious thing. Stealing is a terrible crime. Your father would be very disappointed if he knew what you've done.' I hope the mention of his father will trigger a response.

Instead, he moves towards me, pushes past me and leaves the room. I hear him run upstairs.

'Oh, George,' Helen says and runs after him.

Suddenly I am the one in the wrong. I follow them both upstairs where I find Charlie stuffing his few belongings into his kit bag, with Helen trying to wrestle the kit bag from him.

'You don't want me here,' Charlie says. 'Well, you'll be pleased now 'cos I'm going.'

There is a tussle, which Helen loses. And now we are both running down the stairs behind the lad. Once in the hallway, he turns into the kitchen where Philip is buttering some bread and Jessica is making patterns on her plate with pieces of apple. Before I can reach the back door to stop him, Charlie has run out into the garden. He stumbles a little as he runs across the muddy trenches I have yet to finish, through the gate and into the back alley.

'Stay here,' I shout at Helen, noticing that both Philip and Jessica are following. 'It's easier if I go on my own.'

It's a while since I've done any serious running. Keeping up with young legs reminds me how unfit I am. Years of sitting at an office desk has hardly prepared me for combat. Perhaps Mr Williams is right. The army won't want me slowing them down.

Chasing Charlie down London Road and along the seafront I guess where he's headed. Tidehaven harbour. A few times I call out to him, hoping to slow him down. But it's all I can do to catch my breath and my voice gets lost in the wind.

I slow to a walking pace. If his plan is to track down Bill Marchant again, it will be easy enough to find him. I lose sight of him in the distance, but a few minutes later I spot him, sitting on the shingle, his arms curled around the kit bag on his lap. There's no one else around on the beach. It's still light, although any warmth that was there earlier in the day has dissipated. There's been a high tide, but now it's ebbing, leaving much of the shingle still glistening with seawater. I find myself worrying about him feeling wet and cold.

I approach him and am relieved that he doesn't run away again. Crouching down beside him, I manage to avoid sitting on the damp pebbles.

'Where are you hoping to run to?' I ask him.

He shrugs.

'It's not true that we don't want you. We know it's very hard for you, leaving your family and not knowing when you will see them again. But you will see them again. We just need to be patient.'

His gaze is fixed on his kit bag.

'Is that where the money is, Charlie? In your kit bag?'

'I'm not a thief,' he says, looking up at me.

'It's better to tell the truth. Even if you've done something wrong, at least if you tell the truth we can help to put it right. But if you lie...'

'I'm not a thief,' he repeats.

'Why did you run away? If you've done nothing wrong there's no reason to run away?'

'You don't want me. Philip thinks I'll spoil his fun with his friend, and Jessica hates me.'

'That's not true. No one hates you.'

'She told me so. When she took me to the woods this afternoon.'

'Jessica needs time to get used to things being different. We all do.'

'I want to live with Mr Marchant. He knows about boats, like my dad. And he's nice. He doesn't think I'm a thief.'

I'm beginning to wish Helen was here with me. Navigating between truth and lies with a ten-year-old is so far from my area of expertise that for a moment it's as though I am the child and he is the adult. There's a logic to his argument; perhaps he is right. It would be easier to offload the lad, rather than attempting to settle all the differences that have appeared since his arrival.

'Will you let me look inside your kit bag?' I ask him. The only chance I have now of breaking the stalemate between us is to confront him with his crime and perhaps discover the reasons behind it. I'm guessing he hoped to use it to buy a train ticket to get him home, back with his family.

He shoves the bag towards me and stands. 'Take it, go on take it. Then you'll see. I'm not the liar, but I reckon I know who is.

EIGHT

HELEN

ONCE GEORGE DISAPPEARS OUT of the back gate, I corral the children back into the kitchen where I am reminded that Charlie has still not eaten. I take the rest of the bread and cheese and prepare two sandwiches, one for him and one for George. I have no appetite.

Philip and Jessica watch me as I tidy the rest of the dishes into the sink.

'Will Charlie have to go to prison?' Jessica says. She picks up a tea towel and stands beside me waiting for the first of the washed plates to be put into the drainer.

'Don't be stupid, Jess,' Philip says. 'He's just little. He wouldn't be sent to prison, even if he did something really terrible.'

'Stealing is quite terrible though, isn't it?' she says, posing her question at me.

'Yes,' I say. 'It's a bad thing that Charlie has done. But sometimes people do bad things because they are unhappy. Not because they are bad people.'

She nods, taking the plate and continuing to rub it with great intent even once it is dry. 'So, you forgive them? If they only did it because they're unhappy? And you don't have to tell the police?'

I am trying to second guess where the conversation is headed.

'If Charlie gives the money back I'm sure your dad will say we don't need to tell the police,' I say. 'We all need to learn a lesson from today. If Charlie is unhappy we need to see what we can do to make him feel a bit more comfortable while he is living with us.'

'So you won't be sending him back to London?'

'He can't go back to London because it's too dangerous. Now we are at war it means that the enemy could drop bombs on us and it's likely that London is the first place they'll choose because it's the capital.'

'Charlie's dad might be killed?' Her concentration has now moved from drying the tea plate to constructing an argument. 'And if his dad is killed he'll have to stay here forever?'

I take the tea towel from her, hold her hand, leading her over to the table. 'Let's all sit down for a minute, shall we?' I nod at Philip who takes the chair at the head of the table, with Jessica and I sitting side by side.

'No one knows what's going to happen, Jess,' Philip says. 'We need to be kind and help each other. That's why Mum and Dad offered a place for Charlie to come and stay with us. Like all the other families in Tamarisk Bay. Loads of children have come to stay here. You saw them arriving last Saturday, didn't you? Everyone has to make sacrifices until the war is over.'

'How long will that be?' Jessica asks.

'We have to be patient,' I say, watching the creases appear across her forehead, the bottom lip jutting forward, her fists clenched. My daughter is doing all she can not to cry.

Moments later I am staring at an empty chair as Jessica leaves the kitchen and we listen while her footsteps clatter up the stairs.

'She's gone back into the box room, Mum,' Philip said. 'She doesn't really think she can sleep in there, does she? It would be like sleeping in a cupboard.'

We both wait while listening to thuds and banging in the room above us. Then a clattering sound, before her footsteps again on the creaking wooden treads.

'There,' she says, throwing an old knitted sock onto the kitchen table. I recognise the sock, it was one of a pair I knitted for George that he never wore, telling me they made his feet too hot. The sock lands heavily on the table. It doesn't lie flat, the base of it bulges.

'I was always going to give it back,' Jessica says.

Philip reaches a conclusion seconds before me. 'You stole the money from the tea tin,' he says, moving towards his sister and grabbing her arms.

'Ouch,' Jessica says, pulling away from him. 'You hurt me.'

'I'll do more than hurt you,' Philip says. 'Look what you've done. You worried Mum and Dad and made Charlie run away. You wanted them to think he'd stolen the money, didn't you?'

'I don't like him living here. He needs to go back to London,' Jessica says.

'Oh darling.' As I study my daughter's face I know this is not the time to be cross. I pull her towards me and wrap my arms around her. 'It's a very bad thing you've done, Jessica.'

'But now I've given the money back you won't have to tell the police, will you?'

Before I can reply I hear the front door open.

'Charlie, thank goodness,' I move over to him, wrapping my arms around him as tightly as I had hugged my daughter a few moments earlier. He doesn't pull away, but leans in to me. 'Where was he?' Without letting go of Charlie, I direct my question at George.

'Tidehaven Old Town, down by the fishing huts,' George says.

'We know you didn't steal the money, Charlie,' I say, again directing my words at George. As I speak I watch my husband pick up the sock, turn it upside down, leaving the coins to clatter onto the kitchen table.

'You called me a liar,' Charlie says, glaring at George. 'I've never told a lie. My dad says words should never be wasted on lies. Words are too important.'

'He's a wise man, your dad,' George says. 'I'm sorry I doubted you.'

'Jessica, I think you've got something to say to Charlie,' I say, easing her forward. But my daughter is silent.

Instead it's Philip who rescues us all.

'Sounds like you can teach us a thing or two about boats,' he says.

Charlie nods and for the first time since his arrival in Tamarisk Bay I see a smile spread across his face.

'My dad's a dockworker,' he says, not disguising the pride in his voice. 'And where we live is right close to the water, some nights I hear the ship's horn, real loud it is. Like it's inside my room.'

He looks at each of us, as if he wants to check we have understood.

'And Dad took me down to the docks once, showed me round one of the big steam ships. We went right inside to where the sailors sleep. They have bunk beds and the cabins are so small that if they sit up in bed they'd bang their heads on the ceiling.'

He gives a chuckle, then continues, clearly in his stride. 'Dad had to get permission to take me onboard, but when I'm older, that's where I'll be working. Right alongside Dad.'

'You know what, Charlie,' George says. 'Your dad is a lucky man.'

'Lucky?' Charlie says.

'I've always wanted to work on a ship, any job at all would suit me.'

The fervour in my husband's expression reminds me that after nearly sixteen years of marriage there's much I still don't know about him.

'I reckon our box room is a bit like a ship's cabin.' Jessica has found her voice. 'I'll show you if you like.'

Later that evening when the boys are settled in bed I go into Jessica. I pull back the curtain that divides Jessica's sleeping area from ours, letting the light from the landing guide my way. She is lying on her back staring up at the ceiling.

'Still awake?' I whisper.

She sits up and shuffles over a little, leaving space at the edge of the bed for me to perch beside her.

'Are you ready to tell me about it?' I ask her. I take one of her hands in mine and am reminded how vulnerable she is. At nine years old the world must seem like such a confusing place right now and there's little I can do to reassure her that our lives will soon be normal again. Any sense of normality disappeared the day war was declared and there's no knowing when or if it will ever return.

'I got scared,' she whispers.

'Scared?'

'Yes. I was sure you'd send Charlie back to London if you thought he'd been stealing and it will just be us again, like before. You love me and Philip and you love Dad, but if you need to find more love for Charlie, you might love me a bit less.'

I pull her towards me and cradle her in my arms.

'Oh, darling. That's never going to happen. I would never love you less. It doesn't work like that. Love is a bit like what happens when we make bread. The warmth of the kitchen makes the bread rise and there's even more than there was before.'

'Bread?'

All I have achieved is to confuse my daughter. Even in the half light I can see she is trying her best not to let tears fall.

'Let me put it another way.' I pause, delving deep to find an appropriate metaphor. 'We've been to the beach plenty of times, haven't we?'

Her response is the furrow across her brow, a look of concentration, as she tries to follow my thread.

'We have fun, don't we? Every time we go we add to happy memories.'

'Except when Philip smashes my sandcastles and splashes me,' she says with some indignation.

I smile and continue. 'The thing is we can never have enough happy memories. It's not as if there's only space for a few, the space keeps getting bigger and bigger. It will never be filled. And by being kind to Charlie we can add to those happy memories, for him and for us.'

'Maybe we could make some happy memories for Mr Marchant. He's been sad since Mrs Marchant died.'

'That's a lovely idea, darling.'

'I'm sorry I took the money. Will I have to be punished?'

'Remember what we talked about? That sometimes people do things because they're unhappy, not because they're bad.'

'And you're not cross with me anymore?'

'No, I'm really not cross with you.'

'And Daddy?'

'Your dad loves you very much, we both do. No matter what you do, we will never love you any less. Now I think it's time you went to sleep, don't you? There's school in the morning, remember.'

'And after school Charlie can help me in the box room. I've nearly made enough space for a bed.'

I kiss her on the forehead, leaving her to nestle under the eiderdown. There are bound to be further discussions about the box room, just as there will be debates about George's future role in this dreadful war. But for now I feel an element of comfort that the fault lines that began to appear in our family have closed. Now it is for the five of us to forge a new and steady path forward through the difficult road ahead.

NINE

HELEN

A week has passed and I am preparing Sunday tea. Yesterday Charlie and Philip came back from meeting Ronnie with a great bagful of cooking apples. No scrumping involved this time; Mrs Marley said they were mostly fallers from the two trees they have in their back garden. But there's plenty there to make a well-filled pie. It will be meat paste sandwiches first and we might even stretch to some hard-boiled eggs cut into quarters if the chickens have performed.

I suggested to Charlie to extend the invitation to Mr Marchant and by all accounts it was met with a resounding 'Yes'. He's promised to bring his photo album and I'm hoping we can learn more about his family.

Just before Mr Marchant arrives Jessica disappears into the garden, returning with a posy of wild flowers, which she pops into an empty jam jar and sets it in the centre of the table. In times past I would have cut a few bright orange or yellow dahlias, but this little snapshot of nature is somehow more pleasing. She has even found a sprig of bramble that still carries a few ripe blackberries.

Charlie answers the door to our guest, taking his hand and tugging him through to the kitchen.

'Can Mr Marchant sit next to me?' Charlie asks.

And then everyone talks at once, with George firing questions about Mr Marchant's maritime history.

'Your son was a fisherman?' George asks.

Bill Marchant nods, pride evident in his expression. 'First went out with me when he was just eight years old.'

'That's younger than me,' Charlie says.

'And me,' chimes Jessica.

'After that first time he and I went out together every weekend. Launching off Tidehaven beach, early as we could, depending on the tides.'

'Did you catch anything?' George says.

'Did we catch anything?' Bill Marchant says, chuckling. 'Most times the boat was that weighed down with fish we'd struggle to bring it up the beach. Wouldn't think it to look at me now, would you? But back then I was strong as an ox.'

'Like my dad.' Charlie's gaze hadn't left Bill Marchant's face all the time he was speaking. 'Of all the dockworkers my dad's the strongest. Everyone says so.'

'I don't suppose you've got a photo of your dad?' I say. 'It would be great to see it if you have.' I haven't been back into the boys' bedroom since my foray last week, so I don't know if Charlie's photo still lies at the bottom of his kit bag, or if he has since moved it into view.

Moments later the photo of Charlie's dad is laid in the centre of the table and we listen as Charlie explains some of the responsibilities of dock workers; loading and unloading goods of every kind, checking the cargo, preparing the docks for incoming ships. The words float above me. Instead, I enjoy watching George engrossed, absorbing every word.

Then it's for Bill Marchant to share more stories about his son, as we pass the photo album around the table. From time to time he pauses in his storytelling, his expression clouded, his voice wavering. Each time Philip finds just the right words to fill in the silences.

'You and Mrs Marchant must have been very proud of your son,' he says, as Bill Marchant's hand hovers over a photo of his wife and son.

'I miss them, that's the worst of it.'

'And I miss Dad,' Charlie says.

I break the stagnant silence with a little cough. Faces turn towards me in anticipation.

'Nothing will stop us missing loved ones, but having friends, feeling the support of the community all around us, we can never have enough of that and it means none of us needs to feel alone. Mr Marchant, our door is always open to you. Charlie, I reckon you and Mr Marchant will have lots of stories to share about ships and boats and fishing.'

'Count me in,' George says.

'You're not going away then?' Philip asks.

'The ARP need good men, don't they?' George replies.

I think back to a week ago, the task set by Operation Pied Piper, the welcoming arms of all the families in Tamarisk Bay. I appreciate now that it was as George said - Mr Cowdry was just doing his best. It's all any of us can do. None of us knows what's around the corner, but right now, knowing my husband will be with us makes me feel as if I could take on the world and keep standing tall.

'Charlie,' Jessica says, her voice faltering a little as we all turn towards her. 'I'm really sorry I was mean to you.'

'That's okay,' he says. 'After tea I reckon we'd better finish sorting out the box room. If your dad isn't going to join the army, then there's still a problem, isn't there?'

Now it's Charlie's turn to have all eyes on him.

'Snoring,' he says, winking at George.

ABOUT OPERATION PIED PIPER

AT THE END OF August 1939, when it was clear that war was inevitable, plans were put in place for the biggest and most concentrated mass movement of people in Britian's history. In the first four days of September 1939, nearly 3,000,000 people were transported from towns and cities in danger from enemy bombers to places of safety in the countryside. Most were schoolchildren, who had been labelled like pieces of luggage, separated from their parents and accompanied instead by a small army of guardians - 100,000 teachers. By any measure it was an astonishing event, a logistical nightmare of co-ordination and control beginning with the terse order to 'Evacuate forthwith,' issued at 11.07am on Thursday, 31 August 1939. Few realised that within a week, a quarter of the population of Britain would have a new address.

Many children found themselves in happy, loving homes and stayed in touch with their 'new' families long after the war ended. Sadly, there were unhappy placements too.

Although the south coast of England was considered a safe haven at the start of the war, it soon became clear that it was to be the target for much of the enemy bombing. As a result, it changed from a Reception area to an Evacuation area, with 200,000 children re-evacuated) to safer locations.

Evacuation reshaped an entire generation of youth, yet without Operation Pied Piper, and the biggest movement of people in Britain's history, the death toll in the Second World War would undoubtedly have been much higher.

Thanks to The History Press and the BBC History website.

About the Sussex Crime Series

The Sussex Crime series of novellas recount the stories of several of the characters from the Sussex Crime series of novels. The novellas are all set earlier in the lives of the characters, giving readers the chance to discover more about the experiences that brought them to the point where we meet them in the first novel of the series: *The Tapestry Bag*.

If you enjoyed this novella, take a look at the other short reads in this series:

DIVIDED WE FALL
MORE THAN ASHES
WAITING FOR SUNSHINE
THE HARVEST
CHOICES

If you are new to Isabella Muir's Sussex Crime series and you would like to read more then look out for the full-length novels in the series:

THE SUSSEX MYSTERY SERIES
Featuring young librarian and amateur sleuth - Janie Juke
BOOK 1: THE TAPESTRY BAG*
BOOK 2: LOST PROPERTY*
BOOK 3: THE INVISIBLE CASE*
*Also available as an audiobook

As a reader your words make all the difference
Honest reviews of my books help other readers find them. As an independent author I don't have the backing of a publisher or a team of publicists. I can't advertise in the traditional way, but I do have one thing going for me, and that's a group of engaged readers. If you enjoyed this book I would be very grateful if you could spend just five minutes leaving a review (as short as you like) on Goodreads or your favourite online book review websites, book groups, your own blogs and social media sites.

Thank you!

www.isabellamuir.com

ABOUT THE AUTHOR

Isabella Muir has a fascination for the past – exploring what it was like for families living through the decades from the Second World War through to the 1960s. She is the author of two crime mystery series, both set in Sussex, in the iconic era of the 1960s, as well as several novellas set during the Second World War. Researching all aspects of family life in past decades formed the perfect launch pad for her works of fiction. Isabella rediscovered her love of writing fiction during two happy years working on and completing her MA in Professional Writing and since then has gone to publish six novels, five novellas and two short story collections.
Her love of Italy shines through all her work and, as she is half-Italian, she has enjoyed bringing all her crime novels to an Italian audience with Italian translations, which are very well received.

Her latest novel, ***After the Storm*** is the second novel in a new series of Sussex Crimes, featuring retired Italian detective, Giuseppe Bianchi who is escaping from tragedy in Rome, only to arrive in the quiet seaside town of Bexhill-on-Sea, East Sussex, to come face-to-face with it once more.

Her first Sussex Crime Mystery series features young librarian and amateur sleuth, Janie Juke. Set in the late 1960s, in the fictional seaside town of Tamarisk Bay, we meet Janie, who looks after the mobile library. She is an avid lover of Agatha Christie stories – in particular Hercule Poirot. Janie uses all she has learned from the Queen of Crime to help solve crimes and mysteries. As well as three novels, there are five novellas in the series, which explore some of the back story to the Tamarisk Bay characters.

Isabella's standalone novel, ***The Forgotten Children***, deals with the emotive subject of the child migrants who were sent to Australia – again focusing on family life in the 1960s, when the child migrant policy was still in force.

Isabella posts regularly on her website: **www.isabellamuir.com** where you will also find more free stories to download, as well as the chance to buy all her books direct from the author.

BY THE SAME AUTHOR

SUSSEX MYSTERIES WITH A CONTINENTAL TWIST!
Featuring retired Italian detective - Giuseppe Bianchi
CROSSING THE LINE *
AFTER THE STORM *

THE SUSSEX MYSTERY SERIES
Featuring young librarian and amateur sleuth - Janie Juke
BOOK 1: THE TAPESTRY BAG *
BOOK 2: LOST PROPERTY *
BOOK 3: THE INVISIBLE CASE *

THE SUSSEX CRIME MYSTERIES
A Janie Juke trilogy - box set

SUSSEX MYSTERY NOVELLAS
Featuring characters from the Janie Juke novels
DIVIDED WE FALL
MORE THAN ASHES
WAITING FOR SUNSHINE

THE HARVEST
CHOICES

THE FORGOTTEN CHILDREN *
A story about a mother's search for her child

TWELVE AT CHRISTMAS
An anthology of twelve Christmas-themed short stories

IVORY VELLUM
An anthology of short stories

*Also available as an audiobook.

Isabella posts regularly on her website: **www.isabellamuir.com**
where you will also find more free stories to download, as well as the
chance to buy all her books direct from the author.